Dreamy Rhymes:
30 Magical Poems
For Kids

Contents

The Magic Forest

In a forest deep, where secrets hide,
A wondrous world, both far and wide,
Lives creatures of the day and night,
In a realm of wonder and pure delight.

The trees, they whisper ancient tales,
Of glistening trails and hidden trails,
Where fireflies dance with twinkling grace,
And rabbits run a merry chase.

The owls hoot songs in the dark of night,
Guiding travelers with their soft moonlight,
While gentle deer and foxes so sly,
Watch over the land, with a watchful eye.

But deeper still, where the river winds,
Lies a place where magic finds,
A hidden grove, where fairies dwell,
In a world of wonders, where stories swell.

With wings of gossamer and laughter's song,
They dance and play all night long,
Their tiny lanterns light the way,
Through the forest, come what may.

Now, if you listen close, you'll hear,
The forest's secrets, both far and near,
In the rustling leaves and babbling brook,
Nature's symphony, a magic book.

So, come and visit this enchanted place,
In the heart of the forest's embrace,
Where dreams take flight and stories are spun,
In the magic forest, for everyone.

Amidst the ancient trees so tall,
You'll find a waterfall, a sparkling waterfall.
Its waters sing a melodious tune,
Underneath the radiant, silver moon.

The fairies gather here to play,
In the gentle mist that graces the day.
They twirl and twinkle, oh, so bright,
In the soft, enchanting, silvery light.

And if you look up to the skies,
You'll see stars that twinkle in their eyes,
For this magical grove, so full of cheer,
Is a place where dreams draw near.

So, venture deep, take a chance,
In this realm of endless romance.
The magic forest's secrets unfold,
In its beauty and stories, still untold.

The Little Pirate's Treasure Quest

In a world where the waves kissed the shore,
Lived a little pirate, brave to the core.
With a hat on his head and a map in his hand,
He set off on a journey, to uncover the land.

Through jungles of green and mountains so tall,
He searched for treasure, he gave it his all.
With his trusty crew, by his side, they'd explore,
Every nook, every cranny, every seashell on the shore.

They followed the map, marked with an X,
Through thunder and lightning, and waves that perplex.
But the little pirate, he never lost hope,
For treasure, he knew, was hidden in dreams' scope.

They battled sea monsters with scales so grand,
And encountered mermaids, singing on the sand.
Through caves filled with mysteries and echoes of yore,
They pressed on, seeking riches, wanting more.

At last, they reached an island, untouched by time,
With palm trees that whispered secrets in rhyme.
The little pirate dug deep in the sand,
And there, they found it, the treasure so grand.

But what they discovered was not gold or jewels,
No sparkling diamonds or precious, rare fuels.
It was friendship and courage, and lessons so wise,
The true treasure they found, was a big, heartfelt prize.

The little pirate smiled, his heart filled with glee,
For the real riches in life, he now could see.
With his loyal crew by his side, they set sail once more,
Not chasing material wealth, but adventures galore.

So, remember this tale of the little pirate's quest,
To find what's most valuable, to be your very best.
For life's true treasure isn't found in gold's gleam,
It's the love, the laughter, and the magic of a dream.

The Curious Kitten's Adventure

In a cozy cottage by the meadow's edge,
Lived a curious kitten named Pudge, so full of pledge.
With fur as soft as moonlight beams,
He dreamed of daring adventures and wondrous dreams.

One sunny morning, while chasing a butterfly,
Pudge followed it through the fields so high.
Over hills and under the bright blue sky,
He embarked on an adventure, oh, so spry.

Through the whispering grass and flowers so bright,
Pudge pounced and leaped with all his might.
He met a wise old owl perched in a tree,
Who shared tales of the world and how it came to be.

Pudge listened in awe to the stories so grand,
Of faraway places, both sea and land.
He learned about mountains that touched the clouds,
And rivers that sang their own melodious shrouds.

With newfound courage and a heart so bold,
Pudge continued his journey, his story yet untold.
He crossed a babbling brook with water so clear,
Where friendly frogs cheered, "You have nothing to fear!"

In a meadow filled with flowers, all colors aglow,
Pudge met a gentle deer with a graceful flow.
The deer spoke of kindness and living in peace,
And Pudge felt a warm, fuzzy feeling increase.

As the sun began to set in the western sky,
Pudge knew it was time to say goodbye.
He returned to his cottage, his heart full of grace,
With a newfound love for the world's wondrous embrace.

From that day on, Pudge was never the same,
For he realized that adventure wasn't just a game.
It was the people you meet, the stories you're told,
And the kindness you share, more precious than gold.

Remember the tale of the curious kitten's quest,
To explore the world and be your very best.
For life's grand adventure is waiting for you,
With stories to tell and dreams to pursue.

The Moonlit Lullaby

In a village nestled 'neath the starry sky,
Where fireflies danced and owls said "goodbye,"
Lived a gentle boy named Tim, so small,
With dreams that reached the moon, over all.

Each night, he'd gaze at the moon's soft glow,
As it bathed the world in a tranquil flow.
He wished to visit that distant sphere,
To whisper his secrets to the moon's ear.

One night, a friendly firefly named Finn,
Lit up Tim's room with a sparkling grin.
"Come with me," he said, "to the moon's embrace,
In the land of dreams, we'll find our place."

With trust in his heart and hope as his guide,
Tim climbed onto Finn and took a ride.
They soared through the night, past stars aglow,
In a moonbeam ship, they'd crafted below.

They landed softly on the lunar ground,
Where silver flowers and moonbeams were found.
Tim danced with delight, his spirit set free,
In the moon's gentle glow, oh, what a spree!

A moonlit creature, wise and kind,
Taught Tim to speak with the moon, a magic bind.
He sang a sweet lullaby to the lunar queen,
In a language unknown, pure and serene.

The moon heard his song, a melody so pure,
And in its soft light, dreams began to blur.
The village below was embraced by moon's grace,
As Tim's lullaby echoed, a warm, loving embrace.

With the dawn's first light, Tim awoke anew,
Back in his room, with dreams that came true.
He knew that the moon, in its silent sky,
Had listened to his lullaby, oh, so high.

From that night on, in the village so dear,
Tim shared his moon's lullaby, crystal clear.
For he knew that dreams, like the moon's soft glow,
Could light up the world, wherever they go.

So, remember the tale of the moonlit night,
When dreams took flight, like a bird in flight.
With a lullaby's magic and a heart's sweet tune,
You can visit the moon by the light of the moon.

The Little Star's Big Dream

In a sky so vast, where dreams take flight,
Lived a little star, shining oh so bright.
She sparkled and glowed, a tiny, little beam,
But she harbored a dream, a magnificent scheme.

To be a part of the great Milky Way,
Among the constellations, forever to stay,
She wished upon comets, day and night,
To join the stars in their shimmering light.

Her twinkle was lovely, a radiant sight,
But she longed for more, with all her might.
"Little Star," said the moon, wise and serene,
"Your dream is noble, and it's never been seen."

With newfound hope and a heart so pure,
Little Star embarked on her cosmic tour.
She soared past planets, she danced with Mars,
She wished upon asteroids and counted the stars.

She met the wise old North Star one night,
Guiding travelers with its steady light.
It said, "Little Star, your dream is near,
For your light shines bright, crystal clear."

With a twinkle and a smile, she danced with glee,
As the Milky Way welcomed her, you see.
She became a constellation, forever to gleam,
Living her dream, in the starry dream.

Now when you gaze at the night's embrace,
Look up high, to that celestial space.
You'll see Little Star, in her radiant sheen,
Living her dream, a star of the cosmic scene.

For even the smallest can reach for the sky,
With dreams and courage that never say goodbye.
So, dream big, my dear, and let your light beam,
Just like the Little Star, in the starry dream.

Animal Friends and Their Antics

In a meadow where animals roam,
They dance and play, make a happy home.
Bunnies hop, and squirrels chatter,
In the animal world, nothing's the matter.

The bunny named Benny, oh, so small,
Hopped through the grass, having a ball.
His fluffy tail bobbed as he went on his way,
In the warm, sunny meadow, where he loved to play.

Squeaky the squirrel, with cheeks so round,
Stored acorns high up off the ground.
With a twitch of his nose and a scamper so quick,
He'd gather his snacks, oh, it was quite a trick.

Down by the stream, the ducklings swam,
With splashes and giggles, oh, how grand!
They played follow-the-leader, in a quacking line,
In the shimmering water, so clear and fine.

The wise old owl, perched up so high,
Would hoot and call to the starry sky.
He'd tell tales of adventures, both near and far,
Underneath the moon and its silver star.

The butterfly ballet, a colorful sight,
With wings that fluttered, oh, so light.
They painted the air with their delicate grace,
In the meadow's embrace, an elegant place.

From the treetop, the raccoon peeked,
With curious eyes, always seeking a sneak.
He'd wear a mask and tiptoe so sly,
In the moon's gentle glow, he'd softly glide.

The meadow was alive, with laughter and cheer,
As animal friends played year after year.
In this world of wonder, both big and small,
Their antics brought joy to one and all.

So, remember this tale of friends so true,
In the meadow, where skies are blue.
With animal antics, both near and far,
Life's a grand adventure, just where you are.

12

The Joy of Playtime

Slide down slides, swing so high,
Underneath the endless sky.
In the playground, we're free to roam,
Playtime is our second home.

The sun above, a golden ball,
Casts its warmth upon us all.
Kids of laughter, games, and fun,
Underneath the shining sun.

The slide is steep, a thrilling ride,
With hands held high, we take our stride.
Whooshing down with giggles and glee,
In the land of play, forever we'll be.

Swings go up, then back they sway,
We fly so high, just like birds of prey.
Toes touch the clouds, the wind in our hair,
In the playground's magic, nothing can compare.

Climbing walls, a daring quest,
To reach the top, we do our best.
Hand over hand, we conquer each climb,
In the joy of play, every moment's prime.

Sandcastles rise in the sandbox so neat,
With pails and shovels, it's a creative feat.
We mold and shape with endless delight,
In the world of make-believe, everything's just right.

Monkey bars challenge our strength and grace,
We swing and swing, in a daring race.
With arms so strong, and hearts so bold,
In the playground's tale, we're heroes of old.

Hide-and-seek, a thrilling game,
We call out names, it's never the same.
Behind trees, under slides, we seek and find,
In playtime's embrace, we're one of a kind.

Roundabouts spin, a dizzying spin,
We laugh and twirl, let the games begin.
With friends all around, we're never alone,
In the playground's joy, our hearts have grown.

Cherish these days, both near and far,
In the playground's world, beneath the stars.
With laughter and games, our spirits will chime,
In the joy of play, it's an endless rhyme.

Under the Sea Adventures

Beneath the waves, where coral gleams,
A world of wonder, a land of dreams.
With dolphins, turtles, and fish so bright,
Under the sea, everything's just right.

Down where the seaweed sways in the tide,
Adventures await, let's go for a ride.
With scuba gear on and goggles so clear,
The ocean's mysteries are ours to peer.

The dolphins leap, in a joyful race,
Their clicks and whistles fill the watery space.
With playful flips and acrobatic flair,
They guide us on a journey beyond compare.

A sea turtle glides, with grace so serene,
Through the crystal waters, so blue and clean.
With a flick of its fin, it moves so slow,
In the underwater world, a tranquil flow.

Rainbow fish shimmer, like jewels in the sea,
With colors so vibrant, they dance with glee.
They dart and swirl in a shimmering spree,
Under the sea, where life's a jubilee.

The coral gardens, a vibrant sight,
With creatures big and creatures light.
Anemones sway, their tentacles sway,
In a dance that brightens the night and day.

A shipwreck lies on the ocean floor,
A hidden treasure, we'll explore some more.
With maps and compasses, we search with glee,
For the secrets of the deep, the treasures of the sea.

A giant whale, with eyes so wise,
Swims by our side, a majestic prize.
With a spout and a breach, it shares its might,
In the world below, a breathtaking sight.

As we ascend to the surface again,
Our hearts are filled with a happy refrain.
For under the sea, in its watery dance,
Adventure and wonder, we've had a chance.

So, remember this tale of the sea's grand view,
With dolphins and turtles and fish so true.
In the deep blue ocean, where mysteries lie,
Under the sea, let your dreams take flight, oh so high!

Imaginary Friends

In the world of make-believe, they appear,
Imaginary friends we hold dear.
With them, adventures never end,
Forever together, with our best friend.

They come in all shapes, big and small,
Imaginary friends, one and all.
With giggles and laughter, they play with delight,
In the land of pretend, it's a magical flight.

There's Benny the Bear, with fur so brown,
He never lets you feel a frown.
With a hug so warm and a smile so wide,
Benny's always there, right by your side.

Lila the Lion, with her golden mane,
She's brave and strong, not one bit tame.
She roars with courage when shadows creep,
In your imagination, she's yours to keep.

Ollie the Owl, so wise and bright,
Guides you through the darkest night.
With knowledge and wit, he'll lend a hand,
In the world of dreams, he'll help you understand.

Lucy the Ladybug, so tiny and red,
With spots that shimmer, like jewels on her head.
She brings luck and laughter, wherever she goes,
In your imagination, her friendship flows.

Together with our friends so grand,
We explore a world, hand in hand.
Through enchanted forests and starry skies,
With our imagination, we'll reach new highs.

In the world of make-believe, we find our way,
With our friends beside us, come what may.
Imaginary friends, oh, how they lend,
Magic and joy, in the world they blend.

Remember these friends, both near and far,
In the world of imagination, they're our shining star.
With giggles and laughter, the adventure never ends,
With our imaginary friends, forever dear friends.

Outer Space Explorations

To the stars, we'll take a flight,
In a rocket ship, so shiny and bright.
Exploring planets, beyond the moon,
In the galaxy, we'll dance and swoon.

With helmets on and spacesuits snug,
We'll journey past each sparkling rug.
Through the asteroid belt, we'll safely glide,
In our rocket ship, with the universe as our guide.

Mercury's first, so close to the sun,
A blazing ball, where the heat is spun.
Venus is next, with clouds so thick,
A fiery world, where it's hot and quick.

Earth is our home, a blue-green sphere,
With oceans and mountains, we hold dear.
Mars, the red planet, comes into view,
With valleys and canyons, and skies so blue.

Jupiter's massive, with swirling storms,
A giant of gas, where wonder forms.
Saturn's famous for its dazzling rings,
A cosmic treasure, where beauty sings.

Uranus rolls on its side, you see,
With icy winds and mystery.
Neptune's the last, so far from the sun,
With icy waters, where the adventure's begun.

We'll land on moons, both big and small,
And explore them all, one and all.
With spacewalks and moon buggies to ride,
In the galaxy's wonders, we'll take pride.

But the most amazing sight of all,
Is the Milky Way, like a cosmic hall.
With stars that twinkle, oh, so bright,
In the universe's grand, endless night.

We'll gaze at nebulae, a colorful display,
Where stars are born, in a grand array.
Black holes and quasars, mysteries untold,
In the depths of space, a sight to behold.

As our journey ends, and we head for home,
With stardust on our hands, we'll never roam.
Outer space explorations, a wondrous quest,
In the universe's embrace, we feel truly blessed.

The stars, the planets, and the moon,
In the great cosmic dance, we'll sing a tune.
Outer space explorations, an adventure so grand,
In the vastness of space, hand in hand.

A Day at the Circus

Underneath the big top, the circus comes to town,
With laughter and excitement, it turns our world around.
The tents are so colorful, a dazzling display,
As we gather together, to watch the acts at play.

The ringmaster steps forward, with a hat so tall,
He welcomes us all, with a booming call.
"Step right up, ladies and gents, don't be shy,
The circus is here, reach for the sky!"

First, the clowns burst in, with big red shoes,
They tumble and stumble, with antics to amuse.
They juggle and spin, with painted faces so bright,
In their world of silliness, it's pure delight.

The trapeze artists soar, with graceful finesse,
In the air, they swing, a daring success.
With flips and twirls, they take flight,
In the circus above, it's a breathtaking sight.

The strongman, so mighty, lifts weights so grand,
With muscles like mountains, and a powerful hand.
He shows his strength, with a triumphant flex,
In the center ring, where dreams intersect.

The acrobats tumble, in a daring routine,
They form human pyramids, a magical scene.
With twists and somersaults, they capture the air,
In their world of balance, they've not a care.

The tightrope walker, high above the ground,
Balances with ease, without a sound.
With each step so careful, and eyes so keen,
In the circus's heart, she's a graceful queen.

The animals perform, with trainers so kind,
Lions and tigers, in a synchronized grind.
With leaps and roars, they steal the show,
In the circus's spotlight, they proudly glow.

And as the evening descends, and the stars twinkle bright,
The circus comes to a close, what a magical night!
With memories to cherish, we bid adieu,
To the circus we love, and the dreams it drew.

Remember the circus, with its wonders so vast,
In the world of imagination, it's a spell we cast.
A day at the circus, with laughter and cheer,
In our hearts forever, it will be held dear.

Birthday Celebrations

Today's the day, the sun shines bright,
It's time for a party, a joyful delight.
Balloons are soaring, with colors so grand,
It's your special day, the finest in the land.

With cake and candles, all in a row,
We gather 'round, with faces all aglow.
The birthday girl or boy, in the spotlight's gleam,
In this wondrous moment, it's like a dream.

The cake's a masterpiece, with frosting so sweet,
A sugary marvel, a delicious treat.
With candles to blow out, make a wish with all your might,
In this moment of magic, everything's just right.

The presents are wrapped, with ribbons so bright,
A treasure trove of joy, a pure delight.
With laughter and cheers, we unwrap them one by one,
In the world of surprises, we're second to none.

Friends gather 'round, with smiles so wide,
To celebrate together, side by side.
With games and laughter, and music to dance,
In the realm of birthdays, there's no happenstance.

The clowns and magicians, put on a show,
With tricks and gags, watch them go!
They make us giggle, with their funny flair,
In the world of laughter, we're quite a pair.

The piñata hangs, high in the air,
With candy inside, it's a challenge, we swear!
With a blindfold on and a bat to swing,
In the birthday adventure, we spread our wings.

As the day draws to a close, and the stars appear,
We hold our friends close, those we hold dear.
With hearts full of gratitude, and love so true,
In the world of birthdays, we celebrate you.

This day, both near and far,
In the world of birthdays, you're our shining star.
With wishes and dreams, may they all come true,
Happy birthday to you, today and every day too!

Superheroes and Their Powers

In a world of heroes, brave and strong,
Where righting wrongs is where they belong.
With capes and masks, they take a stand,
Superheroes, with powers so grand.

There's Captain Courage, with a heart so bold,
His shield defends, a protective hold.
He's strong and true, never backs down,
In the city's darkness, he wears the crown.

Wonder Wren, with wings of grace,
Soars through the sky, at a breathtaking pace.
With a lasso of truth, she seeks to find,
Justice and kindness, for all of humankind.

Mighty Max, with muscles so tough,
Can lift mountains and play rough.
With a roar like thunder, and a leap so high,
He's the hero who touches the sky.

Invisible Iris, oh, so sly,
Can disappear, without a goodbye.
She sneaks through shadows, with quiet feet,
In the night's stillness, her foes she'll defeat.

Flame of Fury, with fire in her hand,
Can light up the dark, like a torch so grand.
With a fiery heart and a fierce flame's kiss,
She fights for justice, in moments of bliss.

Speedy Sam, the fastest around,
With a flash of lightning, he's out of the bound.
He zips and zooms, like a shooting star,
In the blink of an eye, he's near and far.

Captain Compass, with a map in hand,
Can navigate, through sea and land.
With wisdom and guidance, he leads the way,
In the world's adventures, he saves the day.

But the greatest power, they all possess,
Is kindness and love, and togetherness.
They stand for justice, in unity,
In the world of heroes, that's the decree.

These heroes, brave and true,
In the world of kindness, they inspire you.
With powers of heart, and courage in your core,
You're a superhero too, forevermore.

Dinosaurs Roaming the Earth

Long, long ago, in a world so vast,
Dinosaurs ruled, from first to last.
With thunderous footsteps, they shook the ground,
In prehistoric times, where mysteries abound.

T-Rex, the king, with jaws so wide,
A fierce predator, in his prime.
With teeth like daggers and a mighty stride,
In the age of giants, he was one of a kind.

Brachiosaurus, tall and grand,
A gentle giant in a prehistoric land.
With a long neck reaching for the sky,
In the world of dinos, he soared up high.

Stegosaurus, with plates on his back,
A herbivore with armor, that's a fact.
With spikes on his tail, a fearsome display,
In the ancient world, he held sway.

Triceratops, with horns galore,
A three-horned herbivore, he'd explore.
With frills on his head and a charge so strong,
In the land of giants, he'd belong.

Pteranodon, in the sky so blue,
With wings of grace, it's something new.
A flying dino, soaring with ease,
In the prehistoric skies, it was a breeze.

Velociraptors, quick and sly,
With cunning minds, they'd hunt and ply.
In packs, they'd roam, a clever scheme,
In the age of dinos, they'd live their dream.

Diplodocus, with a lengthy frame,
A gentle herbivore, not seeking fame.
With a whip-like tail and a gentle pace,
In the world of giants, it found its place.

Dinosaurs, oh what a sight,
In a world so ancient, with days so bright.
They roamed the Earth, in times of yore,
In the land of dinosaurs, they'd explore.

But now they're gone, in the distant past,
Their fossils remain, a treasure that'll last.
In museums and books, their stories we find,
In the world of science, their legacy's defined.

Bedtime and Dreams

As the sun dips low, and the stars appear,
It's time for bedtime, so draw near.
The world outside begins to hush,
In the quiet of night, a gentle hush.

The moon smiles down, a radiant gleam,
Casting a soft and silvery dream.
The bedtime routine, a comforting guide,
As we snuggle up, side by side.

Pajamas on, with buttons so snug,
In cozy blankets, we give a shrug.
With a bedtime story, we start to roam,
In the world of books, we find our home.

The characters dance, in tales untold,
In the pages of wonder, we're unrolled.
With heroes and fairies, and dragons so grand,
In the world of stories, we understand.

A lullaby whispers, a sweet refrain,
A soothing melody, to ease the brain.
With a gentle voice, and a loving touch,
In the world of dreams, we're safe as such.

Under the covers, we close our eyes,
In the realm of dreams, a sweet surprise.
We journey far, to lands unknown,
In the land of dreams, we've truly grown.

We fly with the birds, and swim with the fish,
In the world of dreams, it's our greatest wish.
We laugh and play, without a care,
In the world of dreams, we're free as air.

In the morning's light, we wake with a smile,
After a night of dreaming, mile by mile.
With stories and lullabies, a magical theme,
In the world of bedtime, we dare to dream..

So, as you rest your head, dear child,
In the quiet of night, so calm and mild,
Remember that dreams are yours to keep,
In the world of slumber, so soft and deep.

As you drift away, on a moonbeam's ray,
In the world of dreams, you'll find your way.
With stars as your guide, and the night's embrace,
In the land of dreams, there's a wondrous place.

Bedtime and dreams, hand in hand,
In the world of sleep, you'll understand.
With love in your heart, and stories to tell,
In the world of dreams, all is well.

Rainbows and Colorful Skies

In the world above, where birds take flight,
We look up high, with eyes so bright.
To the colorful skies, we cast our gaze,
In the beauty of rainbows, our hearts ablaze.

After the rain, when the clouds depart,
A masterpiece forms, a work of art.
A rainbow appears, a vibrant arc,
In the sky so colorful, a playful spark.

Red, orange, yellow, and green,
The brightest rainbow we've ever seen.
Blue, indigo, and violet's hue,
In the rainbow's embrace, we find our cue.

We chase the colors, with joy so true,
In the open fields, where dreams accrue.
With laughter and giggles, we skip and run,
In the world of rainbows, it's endless fun.

We imagine a pot of gold, at the end,
With leprechauns and treasures to attend.
In the land of dreams, where stories unwind,
In the rainbow's glow, adventure we find.

With paintbrush strokes, the colors spread,
Across the canvas sky, as we tread.
In the world of wonders, we're wide awake,
In the rainbow's embrace, dreams we'll make.

And when the day ends, and the sun descends,
The colors still linger, like lifelong friends.
In our hearts, the rainbow will stay,
In the world of dreams, it'll never fade away.

So, remember the rainbow, both near and far,
In the world of color, where dreams are a star.
With rainbows and skies, so vivid and wide,
In the land of wonder, let your spirit glide.

Pirates and Treasure Hunts

In a world of ships, and oceans deep,
Pirates sail, their secrets to keep.
With flags unfurled, they rule the sea,
In the realm of adventure, wild and free.

Captain Redbeard, with a hat so grand,
A fearless leader, in a pirate's land.
With a cutlass sharp, and a gleam in his eye,
He searches for treasure, oh, so high.

First mate Sally, with a heart so bold,
Her stories of treasure, never grow old.
With a map in hand, and a compass to steer,
In the world of pirates, there's nothing to fear.

The Jolly Roger, their flag on display,
With a skull and bones, it leads the way.
Through storms and squalls, they set their course,
In the land of pirates, where legends endorse.

On deserted islands, with palm trees tall,
They dig for treasure, 'neath the sun's thrall.
With shovels and picks, they search the ground,
In the world of riches, their fortune's found.

X marks the spot, they say with glee,
As they uncover chests, filled with mystery.
With jewels and gold, and gems that gleam,
In the pirate's life, it's a dreamer's dream.

But it's not just treasure, that they seek,
It's the thrill of adventure, and stories unique.
With sea shanties sung, by the light of the moon,
In the world of pirates, they'll find their tune.

They sail through storms, and calm seas too,
With courage and daring, they'll make it through.
In the pirate's code, they stand side by side,
In the world of honor, they'll forever abide.

These pirates, both fierce and kind,
In the world of adventures, they're one of a kind.
With treasure and tales, their legend's complete,
In the pirate's world, their story's a treat.

The Wonders of Nature

In the great outdoors, where wild things roam,
There's a world of wonders, it's our second home.
With the sun in the sky, and the breeze so free,
Nature's treasures await, for you and me.

The forest stands tall, with trees so high,
Their branches reach up, toward the sky.
With leaves that rustle, in the gentle breeze,
In the world of woods, let's explore at ease.

The babbling brook, with water so clear,
It whispers secrets, for all to hear.
With pebbles and rocks, the stream does flow,
In the world of waters, life's a grand show.

The meadow stretches, with grass so green,
A colorful canvas, a tranquil scene.
With flowers that bloom, in vibrant display,
In the land of meadows, we'll run and play.

The mountains rise, with peaks so grand,
They touch the heavens, where eagles land.
With trails to hike, and summits to see,
In the world of mountains, we'll be wild and free.

The desert's wide, with sands so vast,
A golden landscape, from first to last.
With cacti that stand, like sentinels tall,
In the world of deserts, adventure calls.

The ocean's waves, with endless tide,
They ebb and flow, like a wondrous ride.
With seashells and starfish, beneath the sun's heat,
In the world of oceans, there's treasures to meet.

The night sky twinkles, with stars so bright,
Planets and comets, in the dark of night.
With constellations that tell tales of old,
In the world of galaxies, mysteries unfold.

In the world of nature, so wild and wide,
With creatures and beauty, we'll take a ride.
In every corner, there's something to find,
In the wonders of nature, we'll expand our mind.

So, cherish the outdoors, both near and far,
In the world of nature, you'll be a shining star.
With awe and wonder, in your heart you'll keep,
The wonders of nature, as you drift to sleep.

Silly Monsters and Funny Creatures

In a world of giggles, and laughter so free,
Live silly monsters, for all to see.
With googly eyes and a wacky grin,
In the land of laughter, let the fun begin.

There's Fuzzy Wuzzy, with fur so wild,
He bounces around, just like a child.
With ticklish spots, and a fuzzy nose,
In the world of silliness, anything goes.

Gobble the Goblin, with a big green nose,
He eats pancakes with ketchup, that's how it goes.
With crumbs on his chin, and a hiccup so loud,
In the land of nonsense, he's so proud.

Squiggly Socks, with feet so long,
Dances along, to a silly song.
With socks that wobble, and toes that curl,
In the world of laughter, he's a funny whirl.

Bella the Blob, a shape so round,
Rolls around town, on the ground.
With a giggle and a bounce, she's a goofy sight,
In the world of merriment, she's pure delight.

Spaghetti Sam, with noodles for hair,
He slurps and splatters, without a care.
With sauce on his face, and a noodle crown,
In the land of humor, he'll never let you down.

Pickle Pete, with a pickle for a nose,
He tells pickle jokes, it's the way he goes.
With a briny laugh, and a sourpuss face,
In the world of chuckles, he finds his place.

And as the day ends, and the stars appear,
Silly monsters gather, far and near.
They play silly games, and tell funny jokes,
In the world of joy, they're the silliest folks.

These monsters, both wacky and wild,
In the land of laughter, they're each a child.
With laughter and giggles, they'll never part,
In the world of silliness, they'll warm your heart.

Snowy Days and Snowball Fights

When winter arrives, with a frosty cheer,
Snowy days are here, so crystal clear.
The world turns white, a magical sight,
In the land of snow, everything's just right.

Snowflakes fall gently, from the sky,
In intricate patterns, as they flutter by.
With each flake unique, a work of art,
In the world of snow, let's make a start.

We bundle up warm, in coats so snug,
With scarves and mittens, we give a shrug.
In the crisp, cold air, our breath we see,
In the world of winter, we feel so free.

Snowmen appear, with carrot noses,
With hats and scarves, they strike bold poses.
With coal for eyes, and a friendly grin,
In the land of snow, they invite us in.

Snow angels are made, with wings so wide,
We lie in the snow, by each other's side.
With arms and legs, we create the scene,
In the world of snow, we're living the dream.

The hills are calling, with slopes so steep,
We sled and slide, with a joyful leap.
With laughter and cheers, we reach the crest,
In the world of snow, we're truly blessed.

And when the day ends, and the stars appear,
Snowflakes keep falling, year after year.
In the world of winter, let's make our mark,
With snowball fights, and laughter in the dark.

The snow, both near and far,
In the world of winter, wherever you are.
With snowy days and snowball fights,
In the land of snow, let's reach new heights.

Robots and Machines

In a world of gears, and circuits so bright,
Robots and machines, what a wondrous sight!
With metal hearts, and sparks that gleam,
In the land of technology, they fulfill our dream.

Robo-Buddy, with arms so strong,
He helps us out, all day long.
With tools and gadgets, he lends a hand,
In the world of robotics, he'll take a stand.

Missy the Mechanic, with a wrench in her hand,
She fixes and tinkers, it's all so grand.
With bolts and screws, and a mechanical song,
In the land of machines, she truly belongs.

Sparky the Robot, with eyes that glow,
He lights up the room, with a cheerful flow.
With buttons to push, and circuits to play,
In the world of gadgets, he'll brighten your day.

Digi the Droid, with a digital brain,
He computes and calculates, with might and main.
With numbers and codes, and data to share,
In the world of technology, he'll take you there.

Sally the Spaceship, with wings so wide,
She soars through the stars, on a cosmic ride.
With thrusters and rockets, she'll reach the moon,
In the world of space, she'll be there soon.

And as the day ends, and the stars appear,
Robots and machines gather, without a fear.
They beep and whir, with lights that gleam,
In the world of progress, it's like a dream.

So, keep in mind these machines, here and there,
In the realm of technology, they shine so fair.
With circuits and wires, they lead the play,
In the world of innovation, let's seize today!

Teddy Bears and Stuffed Animals

In the world of cuddles, where dreams take flight,
Live teddy bears and stuffed animals, so soft and light.
With button eyes and furry grace,
In the land of comfort, let's embrace.

There's Teddy, with a smile so warm,
In his arms, there's no harm.
With a hug so tight, and a heart so kind,
In the world of friendship, he's a rare find.

Bunny Boo, with floppy ears,
She brings joy and conquers fears.
With a hop and a skip, she's full of cheer,
In the world of happiness, she's always near.

Mr. Whiskers, with a twitchy nose,
In his whiskery world, adventure grows.
With whiskers that wiggle, and paws that roam,
In the land of curiosity, he'll call it home.

Panda Paws, so black and white,
With bamboo leaves, he takes a bite.
With gentle eyes, and a sleepy yawn,
In the world of peace, he'll sleep till dawn.

Paws the Puppy, with floppy paws,
He chases balls, and chews on straws.
With a bark so loud, and a tail that wags,
In the world of play, he'll never sag.

But it's not just stuffing and fur so snug,
It's the love we share, like a heartfelt hug.
With cuddles and snuggles, through day and night,
In the world of comfort, everything's just right.

As the stars twinkle, and the moon appears,
Teddy bears and stuffed animals, banish fears.
They listen to secrets, and wipe away tears,
In the world of companionship, they're our dears.

Hold onto these pals, both near and wide,
In the realm of comfort, they're by our side.
With snuggles and love, in every embrace,
In the world of plush toys, let's keep the grace!

Magical Creatures in a Castle

In a castle old, where legends reside,
Live magical creatures, side by side.
With wings and scales, and tails so long,
In the world of enchantment, let's join the throng.

There's Dragonfire, with scales so bright,
He breathes out fire, with all his might.
With wings that soar, and a roar so grand,
In the land of dragons, he'll take a stand.

Fairy Flutter, with wings of lace,
She sprinkles stardust, in every place.
With a wand in hand, and a spell to weave,
In the world of magic, she'll never leave.

Goblin Grumble, with a mischievous grin,
He plays tricks, with a crafty spin.
With a twinkle in his eye, and a laugh so sly,
In the land of pranks, he'll give it a try.

Mermaid Melody, with a fishy tail,
She sings sweet songs, with a voice like a sail.
With seashells and pearls, and ocean's grace,
In the world of wonders, she'll find her place.

Unicorn Sparkle, with a horn so high,
She gallops through meadows, beneath the sky.
With hooves that sparkle, and a mane so bright,
In the land of dreams, she'll take flight.

And as the day ends, and the stars appear,
Magical creatures gather, without a fear.
They dance and sing, with hearts that gleam,
In the world of fantasy, it's like a dream.

These creatures, both near and far,
In the world of enchantment, they're our guiding star.
With magic and dreams, in every scene,
In the castle of wonders, let your spirit careen!

Time Travel Adventures

In a world of wonders, where history's writ,
Live time travel adventures, with a thrilling wit.
With a time machine's whir, and a journey's start,
In the land of history, let's depart.

There's Timmy the Time Traveler, with a hat so tall,
He explores the past, with a daring call.
With goggles and gears, and a map so wide,
In the world of time, he'll take you for a ride.

Ancient Egypt, with pyramids so grand,
He meets Cleopatra, on the golden sand.
With hieroglyphs and treasures to behold,
In the land of pharaohs, history's gold.

Medieval knights, with swords so bright,
He joins their quests, in the moon's soft light.
With jousts and feasts, and castles tall,
In the world of chivalry, he'll stand tall.

Pirate ships, on the high sea's crest,
He searches for treasure, in a pirate's quest.
With skulls and crossbones, and maps that unfold,
In the land of pirates, adventure is sold.

Dinosaurs roam, in the ancient land,
He meets a T-Rex, so fierce and grand.
With thunderous roars, and jaws that snap,
In the world of giants, there's no nap.

Space adventures, with planets afar,
He meets aliens, in a shiny star car.
With rockets and lasers, and comets that soar,
In the world of galaxies, there's always more.

But it's not just the past, and the future too,
It's the lessons of time, for me and you.
With knowledge and stories, we learn and grow,
In the world of time travel, let's boldly go.

As the adventures end, and the stars appear,
Time travelers gather, with a hearty cheer.
They share their tales, with hearts that gleam,
In the world of history, it's a timeless dream.

Insects and Bug Adventures

In a world so small, yet teeming with life,
Live insects and bugs, in a world of strife.
With tiny wings and legs so quick,
In the land of mini-beasts, let's take a pic.

There's Buzz the Bee, with stripes so bold,
He gathers nectar, in a meadow's fold.
With a buzz and a hum, he works all day,
In the world of pollination, he'll lead the way.

Ladybug Lily, with spots so bright,
She brings good luck, from day to night.
With red and black, and a dainty grace,
In the land of wishes, she'll find her place.

Caterpillar Carl, with a munch so slow,
He eats and eats, as he'll grow.
With stripes and segments, he'll transform soon,
In the world of change, he'll reach the moon.

Spider Spinner, with silk so fine,
She weaves a web, with a design so divine.
With patience and craft, she'll catch her meal,
In the land of artistry, she'll spin her reel.

Antsy Andy, with a bustling stride,
He works as a team, with nothing to hide.
With teamwork and strength, they lift and toil,
In the world of unity, they'll never spoil.

Firefly Flicker, with a light so bright,
He glows at night, in the moon's soft light.
With lanterns to guide, in the dark of night,
In the land of sparkles, he's a wondrous sight.

And as the day ends, and the stars appear,
Insects and bugs gather, without a fear.
They crawl and fly, with wings that gleam,
In the world of mini-beasts, it's like a dream.

Friendship and Sharing

In a world of hearts, where love's the theme,
Live friendship and sharing, like a gleam.
With open arms and kindness to spare,
In the land of togetherness, let's show we care.

There's Molly and Mark, best friends in stride,
They play and laugh, side by side.
With toys to share, and secrets to keep,
In the world of friendship, their bonds run deep.

Sarah and Sam, like peas in a pod,
They share their snacks, it's never odd.
With crayons and colors, they draw and create,
In the land of sharing, it's never too late.

Lucy and Leo, a dynamic duo,
They help each other, it's how they go.
With books to read, and stories to tell,
In the world of teamwork, they excel.

Tina and Tim, with a helping hand,
They lend their support, it's always planned.
With a shoulder to cry on, and a friend to confide,
In the land of understanding, they're by your side.

51

But it's not just the fun, and the laughter too,
It's the moments we share, through and through.
With empathy and care, we'll stand tall,
In the world of friendship, we'll give our all.

As the days pass by, and the sunsets near,
Friendship and sharing, we'll always revere.
With love in our hearts, and hands to hold,
In the world of compassion, we'll never fold.

Learning and Growing

In a world of wonder, where knowledge takes flight,
Live learning and growing, in pure delight.
With open minds and questions to ponder,
In the land of discovery, let's let our hearts wander.

There's Curious Clara, with a book in hand,
She explores the world, on land and sand.
With pages to turn, and stories to find,
In the world of knowledge, she'll lead the line.

Tommy the Tinker, with tools to explore,
He builds and invents, with a curious core.
With nuts and bolts, and gadgets to play,
In the land of creation, he'll brighten your day.

Eager Emily, with a heart so kind,
She learns and listens, with an open mind.
With patience and care, she'll lend a hand,
In the world of understanding, she'll take a stand.

Rusty the Robot, with circuits and wires,
He computes and calculates, with sparks and fires.
With numbers and codes, and data to share,
In the world of technology, he'll take you there.

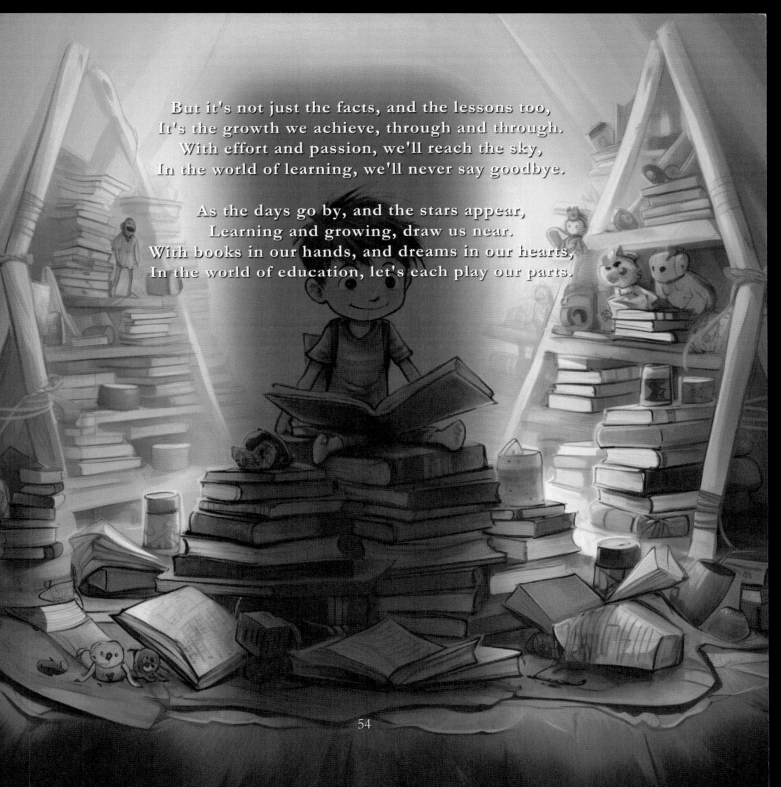

But it's not just the facts, and the lessons too,
It's the growth we achieve, through and through.
With effort and passion, we'll reach the sky,
In the world of learning, we'll never say goodbye.

As the days go by, and the stars appear,
Learning and growing, draw us near.
With books in our hands, and dreams in our hearts,
In the world of education, let's each play our parts.

Family Love and Togetherness

In a world of bonds, where love's the key,
Live family love and togetherness, with glee.
With open hearts and hugs to share,
In the land of kinship, let's show we care.

There's Mom and Dad, with smiles so bright,
They guide and love us, from day to night.
With laughter and stories, they light our way,
In the world of parents, they'll always sway.

Brothers and sisters, with playful delight,
We share our secrets, from morning to night.
With games and adventures, we'll never part,
In the land of siblings, it's a work of heart.

Grandma and Grandpa, with wisdom and grace,
They share their tales, from a distant place.
With cookies and cuddles, they're always near,
In the world of grandparents, we'll hold them dear.

But it's not just the moments, and the laughter too,
It's the love we exchange, like morning dew.
With caring and sharing, through thick and thin,
In the world of family, we'll always win.

As the days pass by, and the stars appear,
Family love and togetherness, draw us near.
With bonds that grow stronger, through every phase,
In the land of love, our hearts will amaze.

Holidays and Festive Cheer

In a world of joy, where celebrations bloom,
Live holidays and festive cheer, in every room.
With twinkling lights and laughter so near,
In the land of merriment, let's all cheer!

There's Christmas Eve, with snow so white,
Santa and reindeer, take their flight.
With presents and stockings, by the chimney's side,
In the world of wonder, let's enjoy the ride.

Hanukkah candles, aglow with grace,
Each night a miracle, in a sacred place.
With dreidels and gelt, and family near,
In the land of traditions, there's nothing to fear.

Diwali's lights, in a radiant dance,
A festival of lamps, in a colorful trance.
With sweets and rangoli, and prayers so clear,
In the world of festivities, let's all adhere.

Easter eggs, in a vibrant hue,
Hidden in gardens, for me and you.
With bunny ears and a chocolate smear,
In the land of surprises, let's persevere.

Halloween night, with costumes so wild,
Ghosts and goblins, roam undefiled.
With pumpkins and candy, in the moon's eerie leer,
In the world of spookiness, let's give a cheer.

But it's not just the gifts, and the treats we share,
It's the love and the moments, beyond compare.
With family and friends, by our side so dear,
In the world of celebrations, there's nothing to fear.

As the holidays end, and the stars appear,
Festive cheer and laughter, draw us near.
With memories to cherish, through every year,
In the land of holidays, let's persevere.

Summer Vacations and Beach Days

In a world of sunshine, where waves meet the shore,
Live summer vacations, what could be more?
With sandy toes and seashells to collect,
In the land of relaxation, let's all reflect.

There's Sandy the Seagull, with feathers so white,
He soars through the sky, in the warm sunlight.
With a squawk and a glide, he's a beach's friend,
In the world of seabirds, he'll never end.

Sandy shores stretch, for miles ahead,
A place to build castles, with shells to spread.
With buckets and shovels, and dreams so wide,
In the land of imagination, let's take a stride.

Splish and splash, in the ocean's blue,
With waves that tickle, as they come to you.
With floaties and swimsuits, we'll ride the tide,
In the world of water, let's all confide.

Ice cream cones, in flavors so sweet,
They melt in the sun, beneath the heat.
With scoops and toppings, and sprinkles galore,
In the land of treats, we'll ask for more.

Picnics on the sand, with sandwiches so neat,
A beachfront feast, it's such a treat.
With fruits and snacks, and lemonade so cool,
In the world of flavors, we'll make a rule.

But it's not just the sun, and the sea so grand,
It's the moments we share, as we walk hand in hand.
With family and friends, by our side so dear,
In the world of vacations, there's nothing to fear.

As the day ends, and the stars appear,
Summer vacations and beach days, draw us near.
With memories to treasure, through every year,
In the land of relaxation, let's persevere.

Thank you for reading!

If you enjoyed this book.
We would greatly appreciate your support
by taking a moment to share a few words on Amazon.
Thanks!

Printed by Amazon Italia Logistica S.r.l.
Torrazza Piemonte (TO), Italy

52464112R00038